FiNG

Papa G

Cover art and illustration by Gary McCluskey

Fing and Ulrich self-portraits by Gabrielle Lucas
Age 7

For my family
Romana, Gabrielle and Alexander

1

Ulrich Von Strudel was born without knees. Now this may have been a huge problem for most children, but Ulrich was the happiest little six-year-old that you could wish to meet. With blonde curly hair, big blue eyes, a cheeky smile, and infectious laugh, he was a joy to behold.

Of course his lack of knees meant he had to walk and run completely straight legged, swinging one leg round and then the other—a strange sight—but Ulrich, a very resourceful young chap, always made the best of bad situations. His mother said to him from a very early age, "Remain positive, Ulrich, no matter what life throws at you. If you stay positive, things will always get better." So that is what Ulrich did. Whenever there was a game of football or tag, Ulrich was always an eager and willing participant.

Now I could fib to you and say that Ulrich was good at these games, but he was not. He doesn't have knees, after all. But as they say, it's taking part that counts, and Ulrich always took part. Sometimes his school mates would let him catch them or let him score a goal—which gave Ulrich great joy and proved to him that if he stayed positive, things would always get better.

So all in all, Ulrich Von Strudel had a happy life, but as he waited in the snow at his boarding school gates for his parents to pick him up for the Christmas holidays, things were about to change...for the worse.

Peter Dietrich, a tubby third year, came running red-faced and sweaty up to Ulrich. "Ulrich, Ulrich, come quickly. The headmaster wants to see you immediately in his office," Peter panted.

"But my mum and dad will be here at any moment," Ulrich said, looking anxiously down the road.

"Don't worry, Ulrich. I'll wait here with your things and tell your parents where you are when they arrive."

So Ulrich waddled off to the headmaster's office, wondering what could be so important on the last day of term.

"Take a seat, Ulrich," Mr. Schmidt, suggested when Ulrich arrived. Ulrich declined, as getting up and down out of chairs was tricky.

"I just got off the phone with your family lawyer, Mr. Snodgrass, and it's not good news, I'm afraid."

"What is it?" Ulrich's stomach was tying knots.

Mr. Schmidt looked pityingly at young Ulrich. "It's your parents. I am afraid they failed to return from their expedition to the Congo. According to their guide, they were captured by cannibal pygmies."

"Cannibals!"

"Yes. Cannibal pygmies. I am afraid your parents have been eaten, though the official term Mr. Snodgrass used was "missing, presumed dead.""

I am very sorry, Ulrich. Can I get you something—a cup of tea perhaps?"

Ulrich stood there stunned. "Eaten?" he said, too shocked to cry.

"Yes, now pull yourself together, Ulrich, I don't want a scene. Stiff upper lip and all that. With your parents gone, you will now become the Baron Von Strudel, head of your father's estate. It's a big responsibility I know, but don't worry, no one expects a six-year-old to run things alone, and Mr. Snodgrass has arranged for your only living relative to assist you. Your great-aunt will be here any moment to pick you up."

"Mrs. Lipstick!" Ulrich shouted. "Oh, sir, can I not stay here at school?"

"No, Ulrich, we are closing for the holidays."

"What about an orphanage?" Ulrich pleaded.

Mr. Schmitt got up from his desk, went to Ulrich, and patted him on his shoulder. "Now come on, young man, I am sure Mrs. Lipstick cannot be that bad."

But Mrs. Lipstick *was* that bad and much, much worse.

2

A black car that looked like the kind an undertaker would drive, screeched to a halt in front of the thoroughly miserable Ulrich as he stood shivering in the snow at the front gates of Wilhelm College. A blacked-out window slid open, allowing smoke to waft toward him. "Get in," Mrs. Lipstick screamed.

Ulrich picked up his bags, opened up the back door, and slid them across the bench seat before getting in himself. Getting into cars was tricky for Ulrich. He literally had to throw himself in head first, then slide across before turning over to sit sideways, resting his back against his bags.

"Thank you for picking me up, Mrs. Lipstick," Ulrich said with a slight tremble in his voice.

Mrs. Lipstick, a vile, thin woman with straggly grey hair and dark soulless eyes, always wore bright red lipstick that seemed to make her yellow teeth positively glow. She turned, sneered, and pointed a long, pale claw-like finger at Ulrich. "You listen to me, you horrible, smelly little boy, I don't want to hear a peep out of you all the way to your house. It's bad enough that I have had to drop everything five days before Christmas and come and look after you. I don't want to listen to your snivelling as well." And with that she turned around and lit another cigarette before putting her foot on the gas pedal. The car lurched away, pushing Ulrich back in his seat with the force of the acceleration.

Von Strudel Manor was about an hour away, but the way Mrs. Lipstick drove, it took barely thirty-five minutes. She cursed and gestured rudely to other motorists that got in her way. As she swerved round corners and overtook cars, flinging her vehicle this way, then that way, Ulrich slid about on the back seat and gave some thought to the terrible situation he found himself in. Eaten! he thought. This could not be. His dad was brave, clever, and strong. He wouldn't allow pygmies to eat him and his mom. No, Mr. Snodgrass had said they were missing, presumed dead. That meant there was still hope. Ulrich remembered his mother's words and resolved himself to remain positive, and things would surely turn out for the best.

3

As Ulrich and Mrs. Lipstick arrived at the front steps of Von Strudel Hall, she slammed on the brakes, skidding to a halt before the large stately home and throwing poor Ulrich off the back seat and into the foot well where he banged his head on the floor.

Mrs. Lipstick got out, slammed the car door, and stood there, arms crossed, tapping her foot impatiently. Ulrich managed to open the door and crawl out on his hands, landing face first in the gravel with a grunt. Then using the car as support he pulled himself to his feet.

Mrs. Lipstick groaned and rolled her eyes. "My goodness you are disgusting." She rushed over to Ulrich, putting her pointy nose right in his face. "Now you listen to me, you little brat, because your reckless parents went swanning off to Africa and were stupid enough to get themselves eaten, it's poor me who has to pick up the pieces. I have to look after your father's affairs and unfortunately you!"

Ulrich tried not to pull away from Mrs. Lipstick's hideous breath as she continued berating him. "Now little boys are foul, dirty creatures who I find utterly repulsive. Little boys smell like fish and poo. It makes me sick to my stomach, and I can smell it a mile away. So to allow me the peace and quiet that I need to run this estate, there will need to be some rules." At last Mrs. Lipstick straightened. She put her hands behind her back and started pacing. "Rule number one," she screeched. "Little boys should NOT be seen and should definitely NOT be heard."

"But—" Ulrich tried to interrupt, but Mrs. Lipstick glared at him.

"Rule number two," she continued. "There will be one meal a day—breakfast, served at 10:00 a.m. sharp. That is it. If you break these rules, you will not live to regret it. Now get your things and go to your room." Ulrich got his bags, his head held low.

"And by the way, I want you to go to the attic. Your own bedroom is far too close to the one I will use, and I would not be able to sleep with the smell of stink-boy." Mrs. Lipstick smiled an evil, sinister smile.

Ulrich's shoulders slumped. The attic room was the only room on the second floor; it was dark, cold, and bare with only a hard bed, a closet, and a tiny window. Forlorn, Ulrich started making his way up the two flights of stairs, which was hard work when you have got no knees.

4

Ulrich sat on his bed stunned, just staring at the walls of the dank attic room, thinking of the most miserable day he was having and hoping against hope that his parents were still alive and would yet rescue him from this horrid nightmare. When it started to get dark, Ulrich decided it would be best to go to sleep and put an end to this horrible day. He got undressed, all except his socks because the bare floor boards of the attic were bitterly cold. Next he pulled on his favourite aeroplane pyjamas from his bag, then went and looked out of the tiny window.

Ulrich was unsure of the time, but the sky was only just getting dark. He could still see the fast flowing Uber River that ran at the bottom of the garden, and as he peered into the gathering darkness, he tried to remain positive. Life was tough enough when you have no knees, but the fact that his parents had probably been eaten and that he had been left in the care of the vile Mrs. Lipstick made it hard to stay positive. But Ulrich's mother had promised him that if he stayed positive, things would always get better.

He shook his head, then went and sat on the bed to take off his socks. He was a master at touching his toes, and getting his socks off was one of the few tasks he found easy. Being that he had nowhere to put them, he threw them at the closet door.

As soon as they landed on the floor, something in the closet rustled. Ulrich held his breath. There was a shuffling, and Ulrich's eyes went wide with terror. Then there was a snuffling. Finally, on this most terrible of days, things got just that little bit worse. The wardrobe door opened a bit, then a black, furry claw came out slowly. Blindly feeling around the floor, it found Ulrich's socks, grabbed them, and shot back into the wardrobe. As Ulrich sat on the bed, mouth open wide in a silent scream, there came an awful, dreadful sound to poor

Ulrich's ears, a sniff, sniff, sniiiiiffffff.

5

Ulrich, in a moment of shear panic, did something he could never have imagined doing— he screamed out for his great-aunt. "Mrs. Lipstick, Mrs. Lipstick."

There was a loud "Aaaagh!" then the thump, thump, thump of Mrs. Lipstick storming up the stairs.

The attic door flew open, and Mrs. Lipstick rushed in, her face almost as red as her horrid thin lips. "I told you, dirty little boys should not be seen or heard. It was rule number one, and there are only two rules. Are you stupid as well as disgusting?"

"But, but there's a monster in the closet,"
Ulrich stammered.

"What! There is no such thing as
monsters," she bellowed. She stomped over to
the closet and flung open the door.

Ulrich pointed in terror at the back. A large,
black eye blinked, looking up at Mrs. Lipstick in

surprise. The monster was just sitting there, sniffing poor Ulrich's socks.

"See!" Mrs. Lipstick screamed, not even bothering to look in the closet.

"But, but, but…" Ulrich spluttered, furiously pointing.

Mrs. Lipstick slammed the door shut and grabbed Ulrich by his aeroplane pyjamas, pulling him close to her putrid mouth. Ulrich was looking straight at her bright red lips and yellow teeth as she spoke in a hiss. "If you disturb me just one more time, I will throw you out the window. Then I will no longer have to put up with your stench."

She pushed him back onto the bed, turned, and stormed out, slamming the door shut.

Poor, poor Ulrich. He was trying to stay positive, but this was getting to be too much.

6

Ulrich stood in the corner furthest from the closet. The sniffing had stopped, but Ulrich felt as if he was being watched. He was scared, lonely, and cold, but he needed to do something. He decided that he could stay in the attic no longer; he would sneak back to his bedroom on the floor below. If he was very quiet, Mrs. Lipstick would not even know he was there, and in the morning he could sneak back to the attic before she got up.

Sneaking around quietly is not that easy when you have no knees, but Ulrich had to do something, so he eased open the attic door. As it creaked, he held his breath. He looked down the dark stairwell, listening for any sign of Mrs. Lipstick, but all was quiet. Ulrich held the banisters on each side of the stairwell and swung both legs to the step below. He stopped and listened, but there was only silence. Ulrich's heart was racing. If Mrs. Lipstick caught him, he would be done for. Ulrich shuffled his hands forward, then swung his legs to the next step.

He continued down the dark stairwell slowly and quietly. On the last step he stopped before he swung out into the hallway and listened. All remained deadly quiet. He could only hear his own breathing and his heart pounding in his ears. He swung out into the hallway.

"What do you think you are playing at, mister?" Mrs. Lipstick's voice tore through Ulrich's head like a bullet. He froze and squeezed his eyes shut, fully expecting to get thrown out of the nearest window. But Mrs. Lipstick kept talking, lower this time so that Ulrich couldn't quite make out what she was saying. He opened his eyes and turned around. Mrs. Lipstick was not there. Light was shining through a crack in the door from his parents' bedroom, and her voice was coming from inside. She wasn't talking to him at all but to someone on the telephone.

Relieved, Ulrich shuffled over to the door to listen better. Through the crack he could see Mrs. Lipstick pacing backwards and forwards, cigarette in one hand, the telephone receiver in the other. "Let me get this right, Mr. Snodgrass"—Ulrich's hopes rose at the sound of his family lawyer's name—"if young master Von Strudel was to, say... have an accident, everything would go to me? The estate, the money, everything? And what is in it for you, snodgrass?"

Mrs. Lipstick stopped pacing, sniffed the air and looked directly at where Ulrich was peeking.

His heart missed a beat, and he gulped. She could smell him, he realised in terror.

Mrs. Lipstick took a puff on her cigarette and turned around. "That sounds acceptable, and you will smooth it over with the authorities?" she continued. "Okay, then I will arrange it. It was only a matter of time before young Ulrich had an accident anyway with those ridiculous legs."

Ulrich pulled away from the door, shocked at what he had heard. He headed back to the attic, thinking that he would rather take his chances with the monster in the closet than the monster downstairs. On the way he grabbed a pen and paper off the bureau in the hall, then he quietly, with a lot of effort, made his way back to the attic. He tried to stay positive. After all, things couldn't possibly

get any worse...could they?

7

On returning to the attic room Ulrich went over to the window sill. Using the pen and paper he brought, he drew.

Ulrich

When he finished his picture, he went over to the closet and threw himself to the floor. He pushed the drawing through the small gap between the doors, then threw in the pen. There was a shuffling from inside the closet, then a grunt and a snuffling and something that sounded like a sneeze. Then the paper poked back through the gap. Ulrich grabbed it and turned it over.

Fing

"FING," Ulrich whispered to himself. He opened the door a little. "You won't hurt me, will you, FING?" he asked.

"No," came a deep but soft reply.

Ulrich opened the door a little more and peeked into the dark. At the back of the closet he could see FING standing there looking at him. He was shorter than Ulrich, about three feet tall, but stocky, with long arms and short stumpy legs. He was completely covered in long black fur, but his main feature was a single large eye that took up most of his face. FING smiled at Ulrich, showing sharp white teeth.

"Hello," he said, and for the first time on that awful day Ulrich smiled.

8

FING helped Ulrich up off the floor and onto the bed, then scrambled up and sat next to him. He was smiling, and Ulrich was comforted.

"Where do you come from?" he asked.

FING tilted his head to one side, looking confused. "The closet," he said.

"How long have you been in there?"

"Forever," FING answered. His voice was soft and smooth, nothing like you would expect from a monster.

"Forever?"

"Yes. First there was nothing, then there were the closets, I have been in many closets, and then you came along," FING said as he stuck a claw in his ear.

"What on earth were you doing with my socks?" Ulrich asked.

"I was smelling them. They were very nice. Among the finest I have ever sniffed." FING smiled and Ulrich laughed.

"Well, there's plenty more where they came from."

FING pulled his claw from his ear, then examined it. "Who was that dreadful woman, and why was she shouting?" FING asked before licking ear wax off the tip of his claw.

Ulrich shuddered, then told FING all about his awful, terrible day. How his parents had probably been eaten by pygmies and how he had been put in the care of the appalling Mrs. Lipstick and what a horrid woman she was and how she planned to accident Ulrich.

As Ulrich spoke, FING listened intently and every so often shook his head in disbelief. When Ulrich told FING what his mother said about always staying positive no matter what, FING could see the sadness in the small, helpless child's eyes and FING thought he could feel his heart breaking.

"What do you miss the most about your mom and dad?" he asked.

Ulrich gave it a little thought. "I miss hugs before I get tucked in at night," Ulrich said, his bottom lip quivering.

"If you want, you can hug me," FING offered.

"I would really like that," Ulrich said. He put his arms around FING, finding comfort in the monster's warm soft fur. He pulled him in tight and for the first time on that hideously dreadful day, Ulrich began to cry as only a lonely little boy with no knees, whose parents had been eaten and whose great-aunt wanted to accident him, could cry—with deep sorrowful sobs and low, heart-rending moans.

After Ulrich had cried himself to sleep, FING tucked Ulrich in and went back to the closet.

9

In the morning Ulrich awoke and quickly went to the closet. FING was lying in the back, quietly snoring. "You are real," Ulrich whispered to himself. He got dressed and by the time he got back, FING was awake.

"Good morning, sunshine, "he said.

"Good morning, FING," Ulrich said. "Do you want to come out and play with me?"

"Yes, I would like that a lot," FING said, and he jumped out of the closet.

FING and Ulrich spent the morning playing Eye Spy and wrestling. FING was surprisingly strong for his size. Ulrich was having a great time, and playing with FING helped take his mind off

his many troubles.

But all that ended with the screeching of Mrs. Lipstick. "Ulrich, get down here now."

Ulrich looked at FING. His mouth turned down at the corners, and his bottom lip trembling. "She is going to accident me, isn't she?"

"She is going to try," FING said. "But don't worry. You do as your mother said and stay positive. FING will make sure that you are safe."

"You promise?" Ulrich said.

"I promise. I have to go and do something very quickly, but I will be back before you finish breakfast. Now you had better go before she gets really angry."

Ulrich threw his arms around FING. "Thank you," he said and then made his way down the first flight of stairs using his swinging method.

When he reached the landing, he stopped abruptly. Waiting at the bottom of the second flight of stairs was Mrs. Lipstick, a sinister grin on her face. Ulrich looked at the stairs. His heart skipped a beat. *Traps!* Some of the steps had been booby trapped. On one stair there was a skateboard. Another two had roller skates. Several had marbles and others, tacks. One step was completely covered in banana skins. It was impossible for a boy with no knees to walk down safely.

"Come on, Ulrich, your breakfast is getting cold," Mrs. Lipstick sneered.

Fortunately for Ulrich the objects covering the stairs were not a problem because he went down the way he liked the best, the easiest possible way for a boy with no knees—he swung one leg over the banister and slid safely to the bottom.

Ulrich dismounted the banister, very pleased with himself, but when he saw how angry Mrs. Lipstick was, he soon wiped the smile off his face.

"Get in the kitchen," she yelled. Ulrich gulped and hobbled to the kitchen. "Sit!" she shouted. Ulrich sat at the kitchen table. Mrs. Lipstick tore off a piece of brown bread from a loaf on the sideboard and slammed it on the table, making Ulrich jump. Then she poured a glass of water and slammed that down too. Water splashed over his bread. Then she took a seat opposite Ulrich and lit another cigarette. "You think you are clever, don't you? You disgusting stink boy."

"No, Mrs. Lipstick," Ulrich said quietly his head bowed.

"Well, eat then."

Ulrich, fearing that the bread or the water or perhaps both were poisoned, didn't want to. "I'm not hungry," he said.

Mrs. Lipstick smiled a thin reedy smile. "Well, you will just have to go hungry then, you rotten little pig."

Then Mrs. Lipstick stood and started cackling like an old witch. "Hahahaahaa! Are you any good at sliding up banisters, worm boy?"

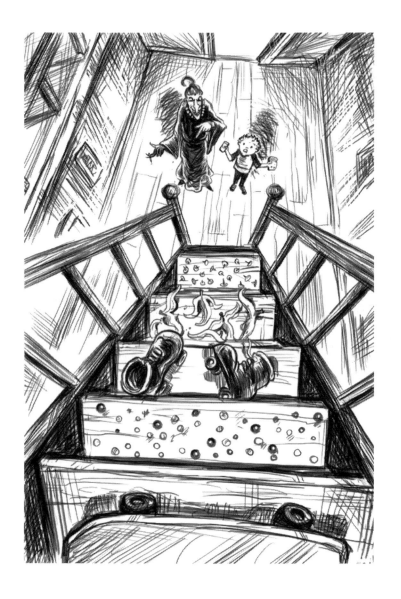

10

Ulrich followed Mrs. Lipstick to the stairs. She could barely contain her excitement and was rubbing her hands together. "Go on then, up you go."

Ulrich looked up the booby-trap stairs and swallowed hard. But then something caught his eye. FING was poking his head around the top corner and smiling. "You can do it," he mouthed, pointing at the stairs. He put up both his thumbs. Ulrich looked closer at the steps. Everything, all the traps had been moved to the middle of the steps. *Brilliant!*

Having no knees, Ulrich could only get up stairs by spreading his legs wide apart and leaning to one side. He would swing one leg up, then lean the other way and bring up the trailing leg. He didn't use the middle of the step at all. Climbing stairs was always slow, hard work, but he was used to it. This would be no different from any other time.

"Get on with it," Mrs. Lipstick screamed. "Your smell is making me vomit."

Ulrich started up the stairs wobbling from one side to the other as he took each step slowly. The first fifteen were clear of obstacles, but the sixteenth had tacks sprinkled over it. Ulrich hesitated. By now he was sweating from fear and exertion. He looked at the tacks. FING had moved them far enough to the middle that Ulrich had plenty of room on either side for his feet. He swung one foot to the sixteenth step, then the other, no problem.

From below a "Bah!" followed him up. He carried on. The next three steps were clear, then came the roller skates on the next two. These were easy since the skates were small and were right in the middle of the step. Then came the marbles. This step was going to be tricky. There was only just enough room on either side for his foot. He would have to be deadly accurate. Ulrich's mouth was dry, and he swallowed hard.

He swung the first foot up. As it landed, it hit some marbles that scattered. Ulrich held his breath. Some fell harmlessly to the steps below, but others crashed against each other, starting a chain reaction across the step. One marble smashed against another, sending it into the next closing the gap on the other side of the step. If Ulrich put his foot on the marbles, he would slip and fall for sure. He'd be done for. Unless...

Ulrich had never attempted such a feat as the one that came to mind, but maybe he could do it. He would have to stay positive for sure, and maybe, just maybe, he could do a two stepper. Ulrich summoned up all his strength and courage. You can do it, he told himself and went for it like a champ. He leaned over as far as he could, farther than ever he had before, and brought his foot up, passing the step with the marbles, aiming for the next. Ulrich held his breath as his foot made the approach. His toe caught the front of the step. He wobbled, then swayed,

"Yes, yes, yes, go on," Mrs. Lipstick squealed in delight.

But Ulrich's foot landed triumphantly on the step. He wobbled a bit more but got his balance, and continued up the stairs. The bananas were a breeze to avoid, and so was the other marbled step, but the last one before the top was going to be the hardest. It had the skateboard on it. There was not enough room on the sides for his feet. Ulrich was going to have to pull off another two stepper. He leaned to his right and swung his left foot up. This time his foot landed true, but now he had to bring his trailing leg up two steps. He leaned to the left and started to swing his leg up. Half way there he lost momentum and started to fall backwards.

Mrs. Lipstick threw her hands in the air. "YES!" she cried.

Ulrich flailed. He was going down for sure. Quick as a flash, a black furry arm shot out from around the wall, grabbed Ulrich by the wrist, and pulled him to safety.

Ulrich had experienced a fright, but he was at the top. He turned and saw Mrs. Lipstick at the bottom, scowling.

She had no idea what kept Ulrich from falling. "Be ready in one hour," she said scratching her head. "We're going fishing."

11

Ulrich liked fishing, but he didn't like the idea of fishing with Mrs. Lipstick. Back in the attic room he got into some warmer clothes.

"FING, will you come fishing with me? Mrs. Lipstick is going to accident me right into the river. I just know it. Please come? I'm scared."

FING looked Ulrich in the eye. "I will, but I will have to stay out of sight. I will be watching and will make sure you are not harmed."

Ulrich put his arms round FING and pulled him in tight. "Okay FING, I trust you. I must stay brave and keep positive and things will get better. Won't they?"

"They will. I promise."

Mrs. Lipstick's horrid voice stopped Ulrich from asking any more questions. "Don't keep me waiting, brat," she bellowed from downstairs.

"I have to go now, FING," and Ulrich made his way toward the stairs.

Ulrich was not worried about the booby-trapped staircase. After all, he could slide down the banister. But he was dreading the fishing trip and what Mrs. Lipstick had planned. When he got to the stairs, all the traps were gone, and Mrs. lipstick was smiling! Ulrich remembered his father telling him that every time Mrs. Lipstick smiled, a fairy died. Now he was sure that story was true. He slid down the banister to where she was waiting.

"Now young man, put on your new boots," she said almost pleasantly, handing him a pair of boots. But they weren't new. They were just his old boots with large rocks tied to the sides.

"I call them pompom rocks. I think they look sweet," she said.

"But—"

Mrs. Lipstick put a bony finger to his lip, silencing Ulrich before he could protest.

"There's no need to thank me, Ulrich. It is my pleasure. Now put on your hat, dear. It is freezing outside." Mrs. Lipstick turned around and got Ulrich's hat. But it wasn't a hat at all. It was a motorcycle helmet with a brick tied to the top! Mrs. Lipstick plonked it on poor Ulrich's head, pulling the strap tight under his chin. "Now don't you look handsome," she said, tapping the top of the helmet. "Okay, let's go fishing."

12

Poor, poor Ulrich Von Strudel. What a pitiful sight he was, stumbling through the snow. Walking in snow is hard enough when you don't have knees, but now with rocks tied to his boots and a brick on his head, it was nearly impossible.

Mrs. Lipstick, on the other hand, seemed positively chirpy and was almost skipping through the snow. "Come on, Ulrich, hurry up. The sooner we get there, the sooner we can start fishing."

"But we don't have our fishing rods," Ulrich said breathlessly as he stumbled once more.

Mrs. Lipstick paused. "We don't need rods. We're going to use our hands. We wiggle them in the water like worms, and when a fish comes to eat them, we grab it and pull it from the water. It's called noodling," and she wiggled her talon-like fingers in Ulrich's face. He couldn't help thinking a fish would have to be mental to want to eat Mrs. Lipstick's hands.

Ulrich kept looking around hoping to see FING, but there was no sign of him. As he struggled towards the river bank, Ulrich did his best to stay positive and hope that things would work out for the best, but he had a feeling of impending doom that just would not leave.

When they reached the Uber River, Mrs. Lipstick stood at the very edge of the fast flowing water. "Come on, Ulrich, come closer. You can't catch fish from over there."

"I don't want to," Ulrich said, looking around for FING.

Mrs. Lipstick dropped the nice act. "Get over here now, you snivelling little weasel."

"No!" Ulrich yelled in defiance.

"Aaaaggh!" Mrs. lipstick screeched as she stormed towards Ulrich. She grabbed him by the brick helmet and dragged him towards the river. "You smelly awful little boy! How dare you defy me." She clutched his shoulders and spun him to face the river. Ulrich looked down. His feet were on the very edge of the bank. Bits of earth tumbled into the river and were immediately swept away by the fast running current.

Mrs. Lipstick started cackling insanely again, "Hahahaha! Are you ready to go fishing now, stink-worm?"

13

Earlier that morning. The Congo. Deepest, darkest Africa.

Baron and Baroness Von Strudel sat back to back, tied together on the dusty floor of a mud hut. They were both desperate as they knew at sunrise they would be cooked for the cannibal pygmy breakfast feast. Everyone from the village was very excited to be eating such dignified guests and had been up late into the night preparing the massive stew pot that they heated on an open fire.

The baroness whimpered, fearing that she would not see her beloved Ulrich again. The Baron tried to comfort her as best he could. Suddenly from a small scruffy cupboard in the corner they heard a shuffling and then a snuffling.

"Who goes there?" demanded the baron.

"Shhhh," came the hushed reply, and out of the cupboard peeked the strangest looking pygmy. He was wearing an odd looking one-eyed mask and, despite the very hot and humid weather, a fur coat.

"A witch doctor," the baron whispered under his breath.

"What's going on?" the baroness asked. "What do you want?"

The witch doctor tiptoed to them and started untying them. "You must be quiet; everyone is asleep, but the sun is rising. You need to get out of the village immediately and head north."

"Why are you helping us?" the baron asked.

The witch doctor leaned over and whispered into his ear.

The baron's eyes went wide as he listened. He grabbed his wife's arm. "Move now!"

14

Ulrich closed his eyes waiting for the inevitable push to certain death. In his mind he pleaded, FING! Please, I need you.

Just then Ulrich heard a growl and turned round to see FING jump from behind a tree.

"What the …?" Mrs. Lipstick gasped in shock at seeing the monster and took a step back in surprise, almost falling into the river.

Ulrich yelled for joy. "FING, you came."

FING raised his arms in the air. "Rarrr," he growled and started towards Mrs. Lipstick. But with his short stumpy legs he was finding it hard wading through the snow, and he grunted as he made his way at a snail's pace towards her.

"FING, oh no! You're really horribly slow!" Ulrich shouted in horror.

As FING continued grunting and making his slow progress, he lost the element of surprise, and Mrs. Lipstick realised that although it was a monster, it was half her size. She took two long strides forward, picked FING up by his feet, and swung him violently, smashing him into the nearest tree so hard that his head came off.

Ulrich stood with his eyes and mouth wide open in horror at what he had just seen. Mrs. Lipstick was laughing hysterically.

From deep within Ulrich something snapped. He was positive all right, positive he had to take action! He clenched his teeth and his fists with pent up anger at all the injustices that had been done to him over the last twenty-four hours—his parents eaten by pygmies, the attic, the booby-trapped stairs, the way that old hag, Mrs. Lipstick, had treated him, and now poor FING! All of it exploded in a red rage. Ulrich screamed like a banshee and ran at Mrs. Lipstick faster than any boy with no knees had ever run before. With his head bent he smashed the brick helmet into Mrs. Lipsticks stomach.

"Oooomppphhh!" she roared as she doubled over in pain.

Ulrich straightened. The brick on top of his head connected with her pointy chin and cracked it open. She stumbled back, blood pouring from the wound. Mrs. Lipstick felt something she hadn't felt in a long time—fear.

"Get back, you little psycho," she pleaded. But there was no talking to the now weaponized Ulrich.

He came again swinging his stiff little legs at her, the pompom rocks smacking into her shins. "Aaagghh!" Ulrich cried.

Mrs. Lipstick stumbled away from Ulrich, closer and closer to the river. When she reached the edge of the bank, she stopped and pleaded. "Ulrich, please stop. I am your great-aunt, your only family in this whole world. Family should be nice to each other, shouldn't they?"

Ulrich stopped and looked up at the evil old hag. "This is for FING," he said and reaching up, ever so gently pushed her on the chest.

"Noooooo," she cried, reaching out to grab Ulrich, but it was too late. She was already falling. There was an almighty splash as she hit the icy water. When she came up, she was coughing and spluttering as she tried to scramble to the safety of the river bank. The current took hold of her, though, and whisked her out to the middle of the river. "You horrible smelly child, look what you did. I will get you for this, Ulrich Von Stru..." And with that she disappeared into the white water of the rapids.

Ulrich turned to where FING was lying on the ground. He felt dizzy. The world around him seemed to lurch and twist and then faded to black.

15

Ulrich opened his eyes. He was feeling groggy but he was warm and comfortable as he lay in his own bed. The family physician, Dr. Boctor, bent over him with a stethoscope to his chest. "He's going to be fine. In fact he's waking up."

The doctor straightened and stepped back, making room for two other people to slip to the side of the bed.

Ulrich couldn't believe his eyes. "Mom, Dad!" he shouted, trying to sit up.

His mother threw her arms around him. "Oh, my brave little boy, I am so sorry that we left you all alone. I won't ever leave you again, I promise."

Ulrich held his mother tight. "Mother, it was horrible Mrs. Lipstick. She—"

"Hush now, dear, we know all about Mrs. Lipstick. The gardener found you down by the river. You were frozen solid and lucky to be alive. He brought you in and put you by the fire and called the authorities. Mr. Snodgrass confessed their whole horrid plan when the police questioned him. He and Mrs. Lipstick will be going to prison for a long time...if they ever find her."

"And FING. Did you find FING's body? Did you bury him?" Tears began to flow as Ulrich remembered the tragic events that took place on the river bank.

"Who is FING dear?" his mother asked brushing his hair out of his eyes.

"He's a monster who lived in closets. He helped me; I wouldn't be alive if it wasn't for FING."

"Oh dear, the gardener found you alone and no sign of Mrs. Lipstick. Just you and some old stuffed toy with its head broken off. Here, look. I have sewn his head back on for you." She reached around and picked up a furry toy. It was black with long arms and short stubby legs and one big round

black eye.

"But… No, Mother, he was alive. I stayed

positive like you said and FING helped me. He

tried to attack Mrs. Lipstick. He stopped me falling down the stairs."

Ulrich's father came over and put a reassuring hand on Ulrich's shoulder. "Look, Son, sometimes when people find themselves in a life or death situation, their minds can play tricks on them. I can vouch for that. It's your brain doing what it can to survive, and this little chap"—his father picked up the stuffed toy and looked at it curiously—"he seems strangely familiar..." His father tilted his head as he looked at the toy. "Anyway, you were in a desperate situation and you were all alone and your brain gave you what you needed to survive. You did well, Son."

He handed Ulrich the toy.

Ulrich looked it over. It did look like FING, but it was a toy! "No, he was real. He was my best friend. He was brave and good." Ulrich sobbed, putting the toy down.

The Doctor returned with a syringe and Ulrich's mother moved aside. "You need to rest, Ulrich. You have been through a lot, and your body is still healing. You were hypothermic when they found you and have been unconscious for days." The doctor prepared Ulrich's arm for the needle. "This won't hurt a bit, Ulrich, but it will make you drowsy and tomorrow when you wake up you will feel a lot better. Just in time for

Christmas Day." The Doctor injected Ulrich with the medicine.

"It's Christmas Eve?" Ulrich said rubbing his arm.

"Yes, it is Ulrich, Merry Christmas." The doctor smiled and started packing up his leather medicine bag.

Ulrich's mother picked up the FING toy. "Here, Ulrich, take your toy and get some rest."

Ulrich lay on his pillow. He was feeling sleepy already but refused to take the toy. "No, he lives in the closet."

"All right, I'll put him in the closet. Perhaps if you make a wish before you go to sleep, Santa will bring you a new toy."

His parents both hugged him, and his father tucked him in. "I am very proud of you, Son, the way you stood up to that vile woman. Tomorrow I want you tell me all about it."

As his parents left, his father turned out the light. "Merry Christmas, Ulrich." His father shut the door, plunging the room into darkness.

Ulrich shut his eyes, tears still squeezing out of the corners. Oh, FING, I know you were real, he thought. Please, Santa, all I want for Christmas is my friend back, he wished, then turned over and buried his face in his pillow. As the medicine took full affect and Ulrich began to slip into unconsciousness, a faint shuffling came from the closet, then a snuffling. Ulrich strained to open his eyes. "FING," he murmured.

And as young Ulrich Von Strudel, the boy with no knees, fell into a deep sleep, he knew for sure, that no matter what life throws at you or how bad things may seem, if you stay positive FINGS will always, always get better.

The End

FING

Also by Papa G

FING

Chapter books

FiNG

Picture books

FING

Printed in Great Britain
by Amazon.co.uk, Ltd.,
Marston Gate.